With a heigh-heigh-ho

Stories and verse for children
by Helen Creighton

Illustrated by Bill Johnson

NIMBUS PUBLISHING LIMITED Halifax, Nova Scotia

Canadian Cataloguing in Publication Data

Creighton, Helen, 1899-
  With a heigh-heigh-ho

ISBN 0-920852-58-0

1. Children's stories.   2. Children's poetry.
I. Johnson, Bill.   II. Title.

PS8505.R44W57 1986   jC810'.8'09282   C86-093463-2
PZ7.C74Wi   1986

PREFACE

When I was young, a long, long time ago, I often wrote stories for children. There were stories I wrote for my nieces and nephews, some that were published in magazines and newspapers and then some that I broadcast in the early days of radio.

The children I knew sometimes gave me an idea for a story or a poem, something they said or did. My niece Lois, whom you will meet in this book, was a particularly happy child. She had such a lively imagination that I never knew what she would say next. Her big blue eyes took in everything around her. She had a rag doll which she carried everywhere, and she also had an imaginary friend called Carey Narey who was her constant companion.

In those days, about sixty years ago, radio was a novelty. As I listened to the Director of CHNS in Halifax talk to children over the airwaves, I thought it would be a good idea to have a program of bedtime stories. So it was in 1926 I became the first "Station Aunt" in Halifax and perhaps in the whole of Canada. We were probably the first station to have children on the air. They would sing and recite verses from dear old Mother Goose and other books.

I continued through the years to keep contact with the young audience. I wrote a monthly column for children in *Church Work* and collected singing games, lullabies and other folksongs in the Maritime provinces. Two small books were published with piano arrangements by Eunice Sircom. These are now widely used in schools.

Those nephews and nieces who helped me in a way to write these stories have asked me many times over the years to have them published. First I just shook my head. I wondered if children today would like stories written so long ago when our lives were so different. Now we shall see!

Helen Creighton
March 1986

Contents

THE SNOW HOUSE

It was a delightful day in January. One of those splendid crisp days with the air so fresh that being out of doors is quite the nicest place to be. It was cold too, but the wind that played about the housetops and ran up and down the streets was gentle. The sun shone clear and bright, and little cheeks of little people looked like so many red apples beneath happy eyes, for weather like this brought colour to even the palest faces.

The best thing of all about this splendid day was that there was snow on the ground for coasting, and ice on the pond for skating. A day of rejoicing for most little people, yet this wealth of things to do bothered Ann Bolton and made her most unhappy.

"If there was only snow," she thought, "I'd go to the field and coast, and if there was only ice I'd go to the pond and skate, but with both of them — oh dear!"

Ann sat on the top step and puzzled. When Bobby Morris saw her there with her skates tucked beneath her arm he called, "Coming to the pond?"

"Dunno." she said. Bobby was too excited at the thought of a good skate to wait, and Ann watched him longingly as his little figure grew smaller and smaller as the distance separated them.

In a moment a group of girls came along. They all had their sleds.

"Coming coasting?" they called to Ann.

For a moment Ann turned to get her sled, for both sled and skates were beside her, but the thought of the pond kept her back and again she answered, "Dunno."

With two lovely things to do she could only sit and say over and over to herself. "Which?"

However it is strange the way things happen, and if Ann hadn't had such a silly little don't-know-which-to-do mind, what followed might never have happened, and that would have been a great pity as you shall see.

As Ann sat there she began to get cold, and being no nearer to deciding which to do, she found she would have to get off the step and move about. To keep warm meant doing something active, and as she could not coast here she had to look for something else. So she took a piece of snow in her hand and then she put another piece beside it. Still wondering whether to go coasting or skating she continued putting bits of snow together until suddenly she woke up to the fact that she was making something. At any rate there was quite a big round place started. Ann looked at it in surprise, and as she looked she had an idea.

"I wonder if I could," she thought. "I believe I'll try. Oh — do you s'pose I could, all alone?" and her hands trembled so that she could scarcely hold the snow.

12

Ann's eyes danced, for do you know, this was the very first time in all her nine years of life that she had ever been left to play alone. This was partly because she had bigger brothers and sisters, and partly because she usually played with a little friend who had a very decided mind and always knew exactly what she wanted to do. So Ann had got into the habit of doing what she was told to do and didn't realize that her mind was growing lazy from lack of use. In fact people said of her, "Yes, Ann is a dear little girl, but she has no ideas of her own," and even Ann herself had grown to believe this was so.

So now for the first time Ann was all by herself, and things began to happen. The snow house grew. It wasn't at all like the snow houses other children made. It was more beautiful, for the snow was just right that day for making all kinds of shapes, particularly where the sun had softened it a little. Ann's house grew to be a palace with great wide verandahs and a flagstone walk and pillars and a beautiful entrance, and Ann looked at it in wonder. The more she looked at it the more ideas she got and everything else was forgotten. She cut windows out with a knife which she got from the kitchen, making them of icicles so that they looked very real, and she even arranged snow at the windows so that from a distance it looked like curtains. A chimney here and there gave a finish to the building, and, satisfied with it at last, Ann turned her attention to the making of a garden. Here she arranged tiny icicles to make dainty flowers, and with a terrace at the front, a lawn and garden at the back, the whole thing looked so beautiful that Ann sat back in happy satisfaction.

By this time she was tired for she had worked very hard. For a time she sat and looked at her house, but she began to think that it wasn't much of a house after all.

"I'll pull it to pieces before the others come home," she thought, at the same time running to the house for string which she hoped she could arrange in the chimneys to look like smoke. As she looked for the string box the warmth of the nursery fire attracted her and she slipped in beside it to get warm. It was so pleasant here that she snuggled down on the biggest chair and in a moment she was fast asleep.

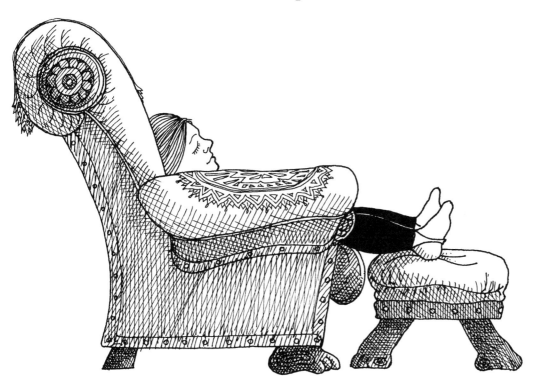

The next thing she knew she was being shaken awake.

"Ann," her big brother was saying, "wake up. Who made it?"

Ann looked up in surprise. For the moment she had forgotten her house.

"Made what?" she asked, rubbing her eyes with the backs of hands that left smudges all over her cheeks.

"That! The snow house." Ann looked about her in confusion. The room was filled with children, her brothers and sisters and their friends, and her own little playmate who always knew what to do.

"If I tell them," she thought, "they'll laugh at me. Why didn't I pull it down before they came home and saw it?" Ann hung her head. She couldn't bear to be laughed at, yet they all wanted to know. Sooner or later it must come out. All right, she would tell and get it over with, only she hoped that they would not tease too much. Her voice sounded very small and thin in the quietness of the room.

"I made it," she said and she looked unhappily at the floor.

Her brother was not to be fooled in this way.

"Don't be silly Ann," he said, and all the children began to laugh just as she knew they would. "She hasn't enough sense to know if she wants to coast or skate."

"Did you sit on the step all afternoon and puzzle? You couldn't make a snow house, silly."

Ann felt herself growing angry, and as she listened to them her temper rose.

"I did so make it," she said, "and if you don't believe me come and look."

Laughing and teasing, the children followed her, and one of them turned on the porch light as it was growing dark. Ann took a little snow in her hands and began to make another verandah. The snow was not so easy to work with now so she could not make the cross bars on the railing as she had intended doing. All the same it was a very excellent piece of work and the other children looked on in wonder. Never in their wildest dreams had they thought of making anything so lovely.

Ann didn't feel at all real that night, for if her father and mother and all the others were surprised, it was nothing to how Ann felt. It was like finding a piece of herself she had thought left out when she was made. From that day on life changed for Ann, and I shouldn't be at all surprised if when she grew up she turned out to be a great artist or a designer or an architect. Anyhow the family took pictures of the snow house, and these Ann always looked at when she felt blue or wanted to do something big and felt she couldn't.

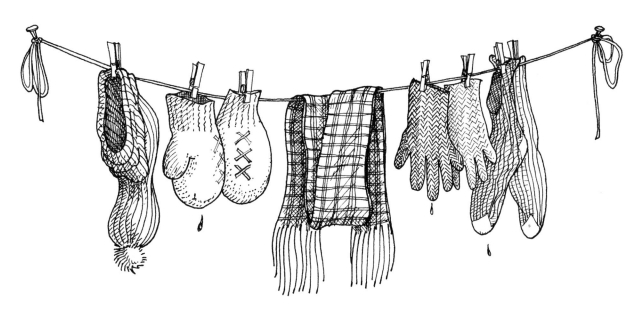

THE TUMBLING SNOWFLAKES

Little fairy snowflakes tumbling from on high.
What a distance you must come from way up in the sky!
I should think it rather fun to float out in the air.
Do you laugh and dance about and never, never fear?

Oh! I like to watch you as you tumble down
And some of you fall on your heels and some fall on your
    crown.
I wonder if it hurts you much and so I'd like to find
If it's a game you like to play or do you really mind?

THE MOTHER GOOSE FOLK

Last evening I went for a walk, a walk,
Last evening I went for a walk,
And as I went onward I heard such a noise,
For the place was full of girls and of boys
And I shaded my eyes and said, "What's it about
And what are the children this evening doing out?"

Then stepping beside me as shy as could be
The figure of Bo-Peep I spied near to me,
And there just behind her was tiny Boy Blue
And the Little Old Woman who lived in a shoe.

"Pray where are you going?" I asked, but just then
There stood up before me the wee Jenny Wren,
And then Jack and Jill with a bucket between them
Splashed water upon all the streets just to clean them.

"Now this is most strange", thought I, "Are these not
The Mother Goose folk? And there are such a lot."
But just as I opened my mouth to say "Why?"
Who do you suppose by Bo-Peep I did spy?

Why yes, 'twas the cock who said doodle-do-doo,
And cried that his poor little dame lost her shoe.
In a tub in a puddle that ran 'long the road
Were the butcher and baker and candlestick rogue.

Then taking my hand in a fashion most coy
Came Roly the Frog dressed up like a boy,
While Mary, her lamb, trotting close by her side,
To poor Simple Simon and Curly Locks cried.

And hopping from fence post to fence post the while
Was dear Humpty Dumpty with many a smile,
And feeling his pulse every time that he stopped,
The great Doctor Foster of Gloucester town hopped.

"Oh, pray, is he ill, Humpty Dumpty?" I said,
For he held in his hand his poor funny-shaped head,
But then laughed the pony, the dear Dapple Grey,
And said, "No, he just likes to go on that way,
For he'd never admit that he might tumble down,
So the doctor stays by so he won't break his crown."

And then what a bleating I heard down the street,
As up came running the baa baa black sheep,
And there they had with them their three bags of wool,
And Margery Daw gave to each tail a pull.

Then joining the company the Babes in the Wood
Laughed at three kittens who each wore a hood,
For though all their mittens they certainly lost
And had nothing to keep their paws from the frost,
They did look absurd with their hoods on their heads,
And I think they all wished they could run home to bed.

Then came Mother Hubbard and said, "See, my dear,
My cupboard this evening was not a bit bare."
And pushing a carriage filled up to the brim
Her dog trotted on with a most jolly grin.

But as I thought, "Now I'll take me a bone
To nibble a bit as I go walking home."
The old woman said, "No indeed, not just yet.
This is for the party! You must not forget!"

So onward I trotted and chatted and thought
What a time I should have with this Mother Goose lot,
For I found them most friendly and jolly and gay,
Oh, we had a great time as we went on our way.

But when we had walked for an hour at least,
The Rock-a-bye Baby said, "Now for the feast."
And as we had then reached the edge of the wood
They all said goodnight, which I thought rather rude.

For although everybody was awfully polite
I thought they might me to their party invite,
But the fat little pig, who saw me look sad
Took me to one side, and said, "It's too bad,
For though we all like you, it's always been so
That just certain ones to our parties can go.
See, there's never a hope while you're flying about loose,
You've got to be printed in old Mother Goose."

MAY

Here is the merry month of May
With a heigh heigh ho and a laddie O.
I can leave off my coat when I romp and play
As I hop o'er the hills to meet my daddy O.

O I'll let the winds blow through my hair
With a heigh heigh ho and a laddie O,
And the soft rain splash on my arm all bare,
He says I can, does my daddy O.

O a mayflower pink will I carry home
With a heigh heigh ho and a laddie O,
I'm a great big man now going far to roam
For I'm sitting on the shoulders of my daddy O.

THE BABY'S SMILE

Across the sea a fairy flew,
Her hair was gold, her eyes were blue.
She still must go another mile
To be on time with the baby's smile.

Meanwhile the baby opened her eyes
So solemn they were wondrous wise
And anxiously looked round about
For something she had come without.

The fairy through the keyhole flew,
(You know they very often do)
And so to end this little rhyme
The fairy got there just on time.

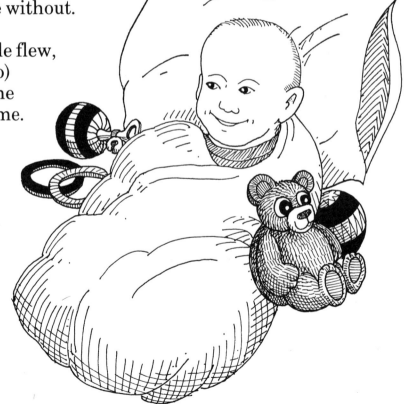

LOIS AT TABLE

Lois has her dinner in a great high chair,
And takes with greatest relish everything before her there.
Her appetite is splendid and she eats until she sighs,
And turning towards the family lifts most solemn, serious
    eyes.

"My 'ittle finger now," she says, "how is it? Feel it please.
I've had such lots of things to eat — potatoes, meat and peas.
Is it quite full do you suppose right up into the top?
'Cos I would like to eat some more, it's much too nice to stop."

So Grandma feels the finger with a very solemn face,
And Lois looks most anxiously, until she finds a place
And pressing it a half way up, she says, "There's still some
    room,
I think you can some pudding take. It's coming in
    quite soon."

"Oh goody," then wee Lois cries, "I'll have to fill it up,
Some more milk please," and with a smile she passes down
    her cup.
And after all have finished, and the finger's felt once more
She says, "There that will do, thank you," and climbs down to
    the floor.

LOIS

Little Lois aged but two
Looks the picture journal through.
Every picture bears her name.
"'ook, here's me! Here's me again!"

Baby pictures here and there,
Baby pictures everywhere,
Babies fat and babies thin,
Babies going out and in.

As she turns the last page o'er
The great book falls upon the floor,
Then another babe she sees,
"Doodness, what a lot of mees."

MARCH

March is the month when the strong winds blow
And we say good-bye to the ice and snow,
When the air grows soft and we know that Spring
Is coming round the corner with a Twing! Twing! Twing!

I like March for the things it tells,
The warm days are coming and the sweet bluebells,
Flowers waking from their long winter sleep
And happy birds a-warbling their Tweet! Tweet! Tweet!

LITTLE THINGS

I had a little thought one day,
I wonder whence it came,
It only stayed a minute
Yet I've never been the same.

I said a little word one day,
Which fell on fertile soil,
It eased a weary doctor's way
And cheered the man at toil.

I did a little deed one day —
A modest thing at best —
It was a nucleus of a song
Which brought a cripple rest.

A little thought, a little word,
A little song once sung,
Oh, how are we to guage the worth
Such little things have done?

THE TREASURE HUNT

Frank and Rae stood on a rock by the shore and looked unhappily out to sea. Their trousers were rolled up way above their knees and one could tell at a glance that they had been wading in water much deeper than they intended. Their hair was tousled and their fingers were black from digging in the earth.

"All my nice old fish-hooks gone," said Frank rubbing the back of his hand over his forehead where it left a great black smootch.

"And that nice golf ball Uncle Clifford gave me," sighed Rae, "and Maggie's skipping rope and Janie's brand new pencil box. How will we ever tell them?"

"Catch me hiding a treasure box close to the sea again," said Frank. "Guess not. Never know about tides. First thing we know the tide will come in and maroon us on this rock. Maybe we'll have to stay her for a whole day until the tide goes out again."

"Yes, and maybe you won't."

The boys looked up to see the merry face of Joe Binney laughing at them from behind a bush.

"What's the matter?" he asked. "Lost your treasure chest?"

"Yes. I say Joe, you've got a funny look on your face. Do you know where it is?"

"Maybe," Joe grinned. "Maybe I don't and maybe I do. But mostways I do."

The boys rushed at him. They had only known Joe for the few days they had been here, but he had told them so much about his life at sea and so many good stories about his adventures that they had all become good friends together.

"Yes," said Joe. "Maybe I do, but I am not telling you. Not until you've worked a bit. I came along last night and saw your precious treasure with the waves getting closer to it

every minute. Next thing there wouldn't be any treasure. Tide would have washed it right out to sea. That's the trouble with you folks who don't live near the ocean. You don't understand the tides."

"So you rescued it, Joe, and what did you do with it?"

"Well I thought you wouldn't want your nice fish hooks to get all wet," and Joe winked.

"Don't be silly," said Frank, and Joe grinned more merrily than ever.

"So I picked the treasure up and carried it away. Now I am going to make you sea-wise."

"How?"

"Treasure hunt. Fixed it all up while you were sleeping this morning."

"Oh, Joe, what fun!" and the two boys jumped up and down with excitement.

"Not so much jumping till it's over," said Joe. "You have a hard morning ahead of you. If your treasure's worth having, it is worth working for. Here's your first clue. It's an easy one to start with. Off you go."

The boys needed no second invitation. They hurriedly put on their socks and boots. Over the sand they ran, then over the rocks to a certain boulder marked by a stick standing in the earth beside it. From the distance it looked like a mast of a ship with one sail, but when they came closer they found that the sail was a piece of paper. Rae, having been the first to reach it, pulled it off and read:

Close by this rock there lie some shells,
Of curious design,
For holding pennies and pins and things
They're just jim-dandy. Fine.

"That's funny," said Rae, as the boys looked around them. There were lots of shells about but none that they thought would do for pennies and pins and things. For a long while they searched until finally Frank kicked the stones under his feet and in doing so overturned a shell. Beneath it he saw a paper pasted and on it the unmistakable handwriting of Joe Binney.

"This must be what he meant," said Rae.

He took it in his hand and looked at it carefully.

"It's just the thing," he said. "Yes, the very thing."

"What very thing?"

"What I could give Aunt Janey for her birthday. She's got the prettiest necklace with all blue lights in it. Look, now it's washed off nice and clean. Isn't it pretty and wouldn't it look nice on her dresser!"

"Hum, I'll say," and Frank smiled delightedly. "Look Rae, here under this one is our second clue."

The boys raced off again. This was not so easy. The tide was nearly out but their route lay over a pond that rested in hollows and over rocks that were slippery with seaweed. At first their goal had looked fairly close, but the nearer they came to it, the further away it seemed. As the water was sometimes over their boots they decided to leave their socks and boots on the top of a rock.

"Are you quite sure the tide won't come in?" asked Rae anxiously.

"No," said Frank. "I don't think it will come. You can see where the rocks have been wet up high and the water's still going down. Besides Joe wouldn't have sent us way out here if it wasn't safe."

This was a cheerful thought so the boys ran on and finally came to another great rock where another paper, looking from afar like a sail upon a mast, stood awaiting them. Taking it off the boys read,

Sometimes when some folks are sick
And the doctor feels their pulse
He says, 'Call the drugstore up,
Give the patient some good dulse.'

Will you like it? No, you won't.
That is may be, I think not.
Still it's good to have a taste
And for boys to know what's what.

At the foot of the mast it lay — funny looking stuff, like leather. Slippery. Should they taste it? Sure. Joe Binney was their friend. He said to. So they took a little, gingerly, carefully. It wasn't bad. Queer. Hmm.

"Like it?"

"No. Yes. I don't know. Do you?"

"I don't know but I think I do. Here's another note. What does it say?"

"It says, 'Time and tide wait for no man or boys either. Get off the rock while you can.' Oh dear, I'd like to sit here in the sun all morning. Wouldn't you?"

"I'm tired," grunted Rae. "Wish my legs were longer. Oh well, come on." So they scrambled off their perch and went ashore again, picking up their boots on the way. When they got to the beach they looked toward the sea.

"Look," said Frank "Our rock's beginning to get covered up again."

"So it is," said Rae, "It's a jolly good thing for us we did as Joe told us. Let's hurry. Maybe there is danger ahead."

"Yes," said Frank, "Isn't it exciting?"

To follow the next clue was not so difficult. It took them along the level beach and soon they were racing one another and forgetting they were tired. When they came to their stop they found a sail flying from a little wooden boat Joe had made for them. In fact there were two wooden boats. On one of the sails was written:

Put your boots on here or you
Will be caught by cares and woes,
For these crabs you see lying here
Love to cling to people's toes.

The boys laughed and hastened to obey.

"How did he know we'd have our boots off?" they asked. "Isn't he wonderful, our Joe? Look at the crabs. Aren't they funny looking things? Does he say to do anything with them?

"No, he says to go out on that pebbly bit and dig."

"What for? Treasure?"

"For clams."

So the boys went out to the pebbly bit and again removed their boots and socks. Then digging in the soft sand they found dozens of clams in shells. Obeying orders, they filled their pocket hankerchiefs and their hats and took away as many as they could carry. Perhaps this took longer than Joe Binney thought for they got so excited in their digging that the sea was up to them before they noticed it and one boot all but washed away.

By this time they were getting hungry so they hurried off to their next clue. Here they found a note saying.

Gather sticks of dry driftwood
For a fire they are good.
Matches on the shelf are set.
Can you get your fire lit?

A tiny bonfire place enclosed with rocks awaited them. When the fire was going, they opened another note set on a match and read.

Pot with water you will find
If you look this ledge behind.
Wash your clams, When water's hot
Cook them in this nice iron pot.

Then the grinning face of Joe Binney appeared from behind a bush.

"Having a good time?" he asked. "Like to invite me to the clam feed?"

And Joe sat on the sand behind them and told them how to do it. Never had the boys tasted anything so good, nor had they cooked anything on the beach before, and when at length they finished their meal and found their treasure box on a high ledge of rock in a cave nearby, they thought this was the best morning they had ever spent.

When their holiday was over and they went home, they took many treasures of the sea with them which they would never have seen if it had not been for their friend, Joe Binney.

THE FIRE ENGINE

Some people get excited when the moon comes
    in the sky,
And others think it lots of fun to watch a
    parade go by,
But I don't pay attention to such things so mild
    and meek,
I'd rather watch the fire engine racing down
    the street.

Some people like to play at cards, and some go
    out to tea,
And some sit up at concerts, though how they
    do beats me,
But if any people 'round this town would like to
    give a treat,
They'll call the fire engine out to race along the
    street.

Some boys I know stay in the house and read
 their books all day
Or else sit stiffly on a bench and learn a piece
 to play,
But though I like that too at times, I thrill from
 head to feet
Whene'er the fire engine comes a-racing down
 the street.

'Course girls are awful scaredy and make a
 fuss and scream,
They make me tired the way they like to sit
 about and dream,
They're either awful tomboys or they're prim,
 you know, and neat,
And don't they hate the fire engine racing
 down the street?

Oh, boys and girls, and grown-ups too, play
 what you like to play,
But if you ever see me run, please don't get in
 my way,
For I'd walk a thousand miles and wear the
 skin right off my feet
To see the fire engine racing, racing down the
 street.

54

The End